To all the dedicated teachers
of the world—thank you.

Sindy McKay

For Kristen:
Coincidentally Clever,
Continuously Cool,
Considerably Crazy,

Bob

Parent's Introduction

We Both Read is the first series of books designed to invite parents and children to share the reading of a story by taking turns reading aloud. This "shared reading" innovation, which was developed in conjunction with early reading specialists, invites parents to read the more sophisticated text on the left-hand pages, while children are encouraged to read the right-hand pages, which have been written at one of three early reading levels.

Reading aloud is one of the most important activities parents can share with their child to assist their reading development. However, *We Both Read* goes beyond reading *to* a child and allows parents to share reading *with* a child. *We Both Read* is so powerful and effective because it combines two key elements in learning: "showing" (the parent reads) and "doing" (the child reads). The result is not only faster reading development for the child, but a much more enjoyable and enriching experience for both!

Most of the words used in the child's text should be familiar to them. Others can easily be sounded out. You may find it helpful to read the entire book aloud yourself the first time, then invite your child to participate on the second reading. Also note that the parent's text is preceded by a "talking parent" icon: ; and the child's text is preceded by a "talking child" icon:

We Both Read books is a fun, easy way to encourage and help your child to read—and a wonderful way to start your child off on a lifetime of reading enjoyment!

We Both Read: June's Tune

Published by Treasure Bay, Inc.
17 Parkgrove Drive
South San Francisco, CA 94080 USA

PRINTED IN SINGAPORE

Library of Congress Catalog Card Number: 00 131594

Hardcover ISBN: 1-891327-25-9
Paperback ISBN: 1-891327-26-7

FIRST EDITION

We Both Read® Books
Patent No. 5,957,693

Visit us online at:
www.webothread.com

June's Tune

By Sindy McKay
Illustrated by Bob Staake

TREASURE BAY

One lazy summer day, June woke up with a song in her head. She didn't know where it came from. She just woke up and there it was.

June called her tune . . .

. . . June's Tune.

June hummed her tune all morning long.
She hummed it loud and she hummed it soft.
She hummed it high and she hummed it low.
She hummed it with a narrow grin.
She hummed it with a big . . .

. . . wide smile.

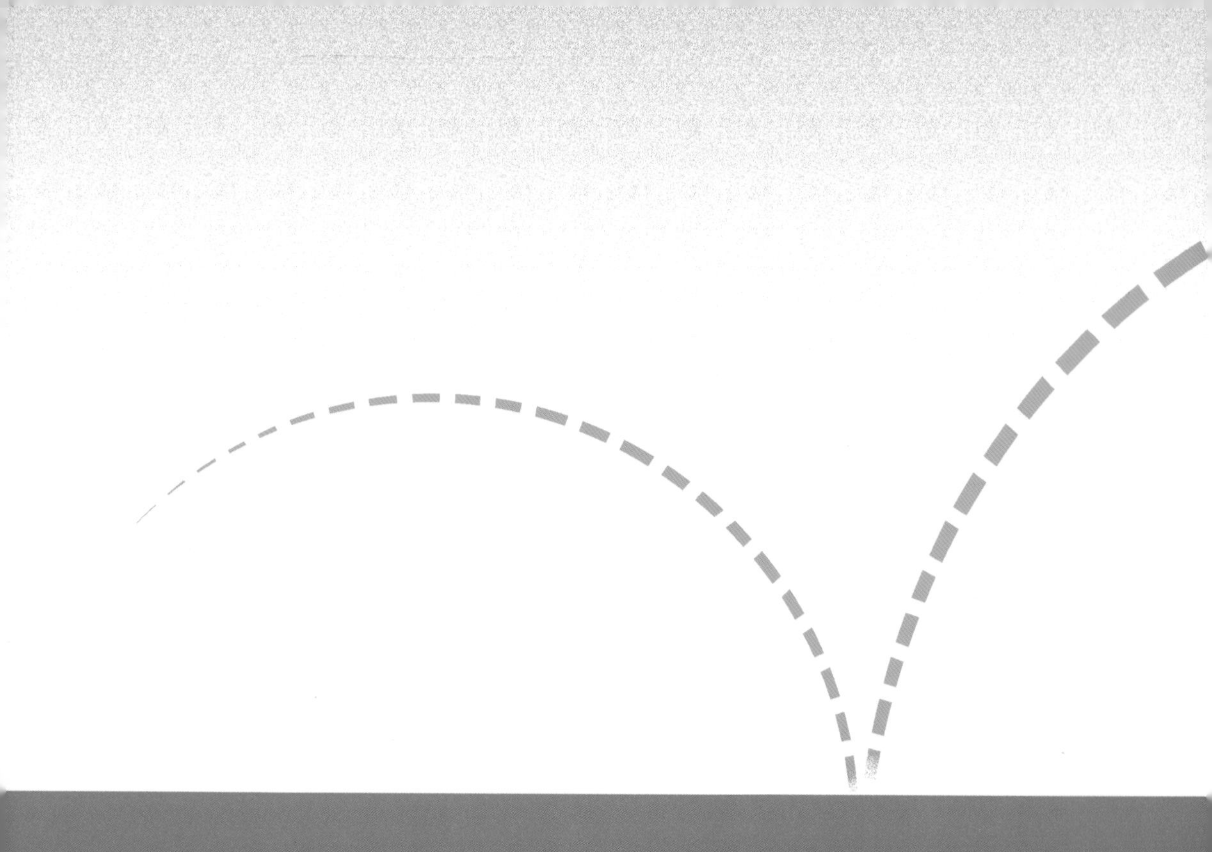

June loved her tune. It couldn't be better. Unless, of course, the tune had some words.

"Yes!" cried June."My tune should have words. Someone should write some. And that someone should . . .

. . . be me!”

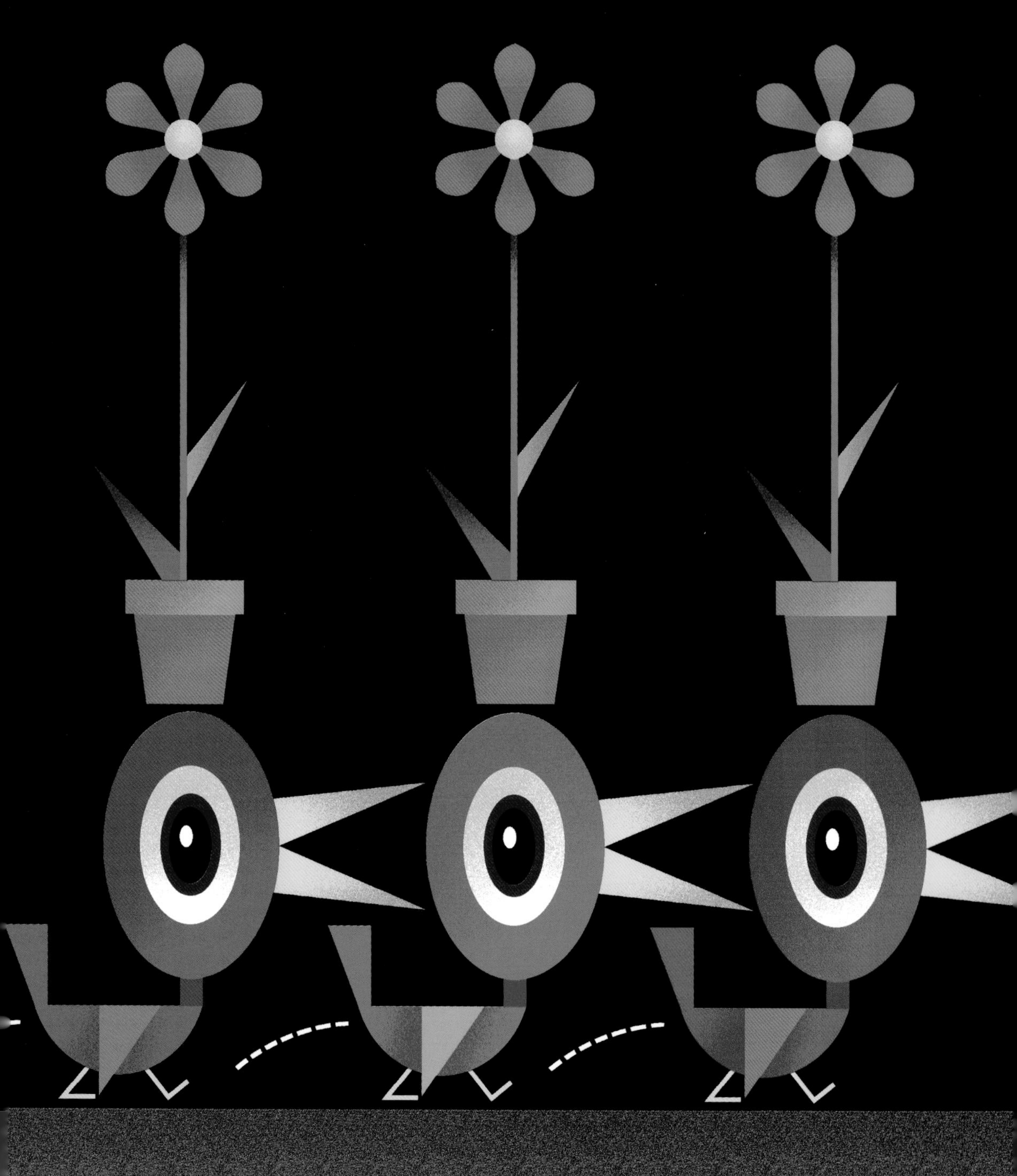

June thought her tune could be about flowers.
She thought her tune could be about birds.
She thought it could be about a deer near her ear.
She thought it could be about . . .

. . . a rose by her nose.

S.S. June

June thought it could be about chocolate ice cream and how yummy it tastes on a hot summer day. Then she changed her mind and thought it might be the directions to bake . . .

. . . a cake by a lake.

June's tune could be about so many things! It could be about kittens or lambs or goats. It could be about skateboards or . . .

. . . bikes or kites.

Joe grabbed June's bike and hollered, "STOP!"

Then Joe told June her tune was great, but the words she was singing were no fun at all.

"In fact," said Joe, "they are . . .

. . . more like a bore."

Joe felt the words should be really exciting and tell the tale of a dinosaur with great big teeth. Or the adventures of a super guy with a magic . . .

. . . cape and rake.

June just laughed and shook her head. June's Tune wasn't that kind of song at all! The tune was sweet and the words should be too. Sweet enough to put . . .

. . . sheep to sleep.

Joe insisted that June was wrong. Her tune was made for excitement and thrills! It was made for a story about big giant bugs. Or bees so huge you could . . .

. . . drive in the hive!

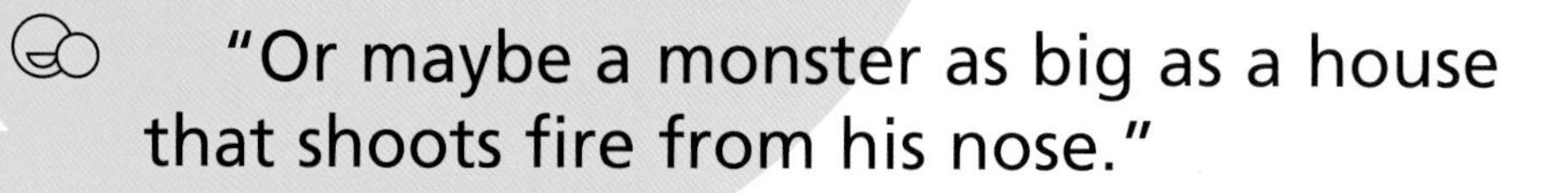

"Or maybe a monster as big as a house that shoots fire from his nose."

June said that was fine, except for the fire. This monster should be sweet. Like a . . .

. . . brute with a flute.

Joe rolled his eyes and said that was dumb, so June said her tune would NOT be about monsters.

It would be about horses and boyfriends and love. It would be about weddings and . . .

. . . a bride
that can ride.

June and Joe argued, then argued some more. They'd be arguing STILL if Mike didn't speak up.

Mike was a good friend of both . . .

. . . June and Joe.

Mike asked what his friends were fighting about and they told him they were fighting over the words for June's Tune.

Then Joe and June asked, which words did . . .

. . . Mike like?

"I like them all," Mike said with a smile. "They ALL sound like fun. If you put them together, you could make a great song!"

"June's Tune could be about a rose with a nose . . .

. . . on a bike
with a rake."

Joe and June laughed to think of a rose with a nose. They asked Mike what else June's Tune could be about.

Mike replied, "How about a huge dinosaur who likes to fly kites and his very best friend . . .

. . . a goat with a flute."

Now June and Joe were starting to catch on!

Joe said they could write about a brute in a cape that rides a big skateboard and eats . . .

. . . ice cream and sheep.

June could barely breathe, she was laughing so much. But she stopped long enough to come up with some words about a bride from a hive who . . .

. . . drives a big cake.

June and Joe and Mike laughed so hard that tears rolled down their cheeks! They all agreed that this song was great fun. And fun was exactly the point of . . .

. . . June's Tune!

If you liked
***June's Tune*, here are two other**
***We Both Read*™ Books you are sure to enjoy!**

Kibu is a young member of the Masai tribe in Africa. When Kibu is told he is too small to go on the lion hunt, he decides to prove that he too can be a mighty lion hunter. He sets off into the wilderness to find the biggest lion of all, Father Lion. With the help of some animal friends he meets along the way, Kibu hopes to outsmart and capture Father Lion.

A very whimsical tale of a boy and his dog and their fantastic dreamland adventures. This delightful tale features fun and easy to read text for the very beginning reader, such as "pigs that dig", "fish on a dish", and a "dog on a frog." Both children and their parents will love this newest addition to the We Both Read series!

To see all the We Both Read books that are available,
just go online to **www.webothread.com**